To Sir Robbo
—M.R.

To Sir Sonny
—F.B.

Dial Books for Young Readers
Penguin Young Readers Group
An imprint of Penguin Random House LLC
375 Hudson Street
New York, NY 10014

Library of Congress Cataloging-in-Publication Data

Names: Robinson, Michelle (Michelle Jane), date. | Blunt, Fred, illustrator.
Title: The forgetful knight / by Michelle Robinson and Fred Blunt.
Description: New York : Dial Books for Young Readers, [2016] | Summary: "A forgetful narrator tries to tell the tale of a knight's duel with a dragon, and remembers a very important thing along the way"—Provided by publisher.
Identifiers: LCCN 2015019779 | ISBN 9780803740679 (hardcover)
Subjects: | CYAC: Stories in rhyme. | Knights and knighthood—Fiction. | Dragons—Fiction. | Memory—Fiction. | Humorous stories.
Classification: LCC PZ8.3.R5814 Fo 2016 | DDC [E]—dc23
LC record available at http://lccn.loc.gov/2015019779

Manufactured in China on acid-free paper
10 9 8 7 6 5 4 3 2 1

Designed by Mina Chung • Text set in Mrs. Ant
This art was created using HB pencils, cheap paper, and a Mac!

by Michelle Robinson and Fred Blunt

THE FORGETFUL KNIGHT

Dial Books for Young Readers

Once upon an olden day
A knight in armor rode away.

Then again ...

he had no horse.
Did I say "rode"?

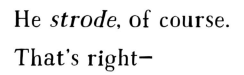

He *strode*, of course.
That's right—

he *strode* across the land,

with half a sandwich in his hand?

Meow

A sword! That's what I meant to say,
because the **knight** was on his way ...

to what?

A party?

Movie night?

Hang on, I know—

a Daring Fight!
He had to slay a whatitsname.

A thingybob?

Not that . . . Too tame.

purrr

What's scaly, HUGE,
and breathes out flame?

A DRAGON!

That's it—big and green.
But mostly it was just plain mean.

It liked to snaffle people's pets
(it had a field day at the vet's),

and worst of all, this dragon ate
Sir Clopalot, the knight's best mate.

Sir Clop was ...

handsome?

Hairy?

Tall?

I'm sorry, I just can't recall.
But he was special—that's a fact.
And so our knight just had to act.

"I miss my friend!" he cried. And so:
"That nasty dragon has to go!"

At last he found the dragon's cave,
and strode right in, for he was brave.

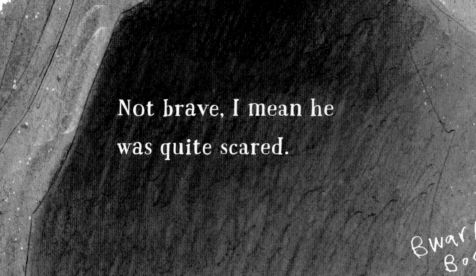

Not brave, I mean he
was quite scared.

Go in the cave?
He never dared!

He grabbed his phone, he dialed home,

Said, "Mommy, help! I'm all alone!"

No, no! He was too bold for that,
I'm sure he would have fought that ... cat?

I mean ...

dragon.

He did! He went and fought the beast!

Or was it that he bought a feast?
I'm hungry. Curly fries for me.
And you? The story? Right, let's see ...

"You ate my friend!"
the brave knight said.
But hang on—*was* Sir Cloppy dead?

Amazingly, from far away,
There came a faint and friendly...

Neigh

The knight's best friend was Clop the *horse*!
(I knew that all along, of course.)

The knight attacked!
The dragon **COUGHED!**

Our hero held his ~~sandwich~~ sword aloft.

He wasn't pulling *any* punches:
Out came **ALL** the dragon's lunches.

"Say sorry!" our brave knight demanded.
The dragon, feeling reprimanded,
chose to set his pants alight.

That did it.

What an angry knight!

He **BASHED** the dragon on the head.

The dragon **BASHED** him back.

RAAAA

BAT

They're dead.
The end.

Hang on—the dragon didn't die.
He got told off and had a cry,
and never ate a pet again
(well, just a small one now and then).

I think the knight survived as well.

It's really very hard to tell
since *someone* lost his memory ...

The knight?

That's right!

The knight was ...